The Bear, the Bat and the Dove
3 stories from Aesop

as told by Rob Cleveland
illustrated by Baird Hoffmire

The Bear
and the Two
Travelers

Two men were walking together in the woods,
when a bear suddenly met them on their path.

The two men ran to a nearby tree and started to climb.

One man was able to climb the tree, but left his friend on the ground.

Seeing that the bear was about to attack him, he laid down flat on the ground.

The bear came up to the man on the ground and sniffed him and bumped him with his large snout. The man on the ground laid still and pretended to be dead.

After a few moments, the bear leaned over to the man's ear and then walked away.

When the bear was gone, the other man climbed
down from the tree and went to his friend and
asked him what the bear had whispered in his ear.

"He gave me some advice," said the man.
"What advice?" asked his friend. "He said,
never travel with a friend who deserts you at
the first sign of danger."

Why Bat Flies at Night

Many, many years ago, there was a war between the animals of the land and the birds of the sky. No one knows how the war started.

As Bat hung in a tree and watched the battle, he could not decide which side to join. When it seemed that the birds would win the war, Bat flew to the side of the birds.

"Why are you here?" said the birds. "You are a land animal!"
"I am one of you, look at my wings," said Bat.
The birds accepted him as one of them.

As the war went on, the animals of the land started to win. Bat flew to the land animals. "Why are you here?" growled the animals. "You are not an animal, you are a bird."

"Wait, I am one of you. Look at my teeth and fur," said Bat. He grinned at the animals to show them his teeth, and he even let them feel his fur. The animals accepted him as one of them.

That is how it went for the rest of the war.
Bat would always join the side which seemed
to be winning.

One day the war was over. There was peace between the animals of the land and the birds of the sky.

When Bat arrived, he knew he could not sit
with either side. "Come brother, sit with us,"
said the birds. "No brother, come sit with us,"
growled the animals.

All of a sudden, the animals of the land and the birds of the sky realized what Bat had done. They chased him away.
Bat flew into a dark cave to hide.

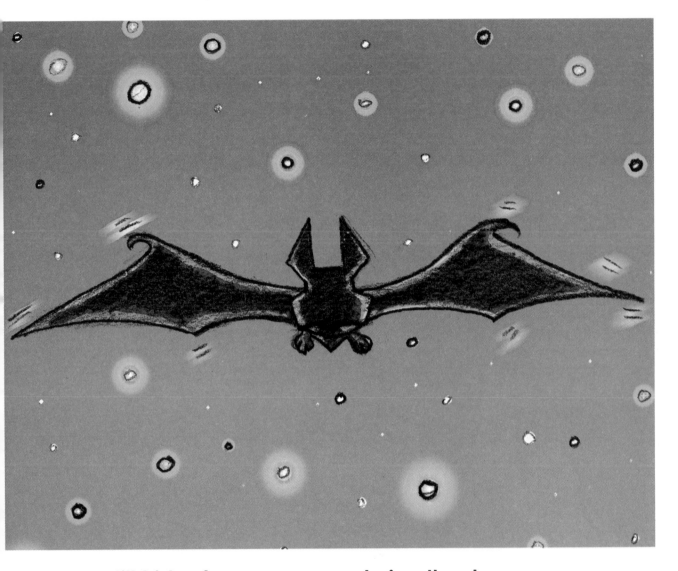

He still hides from everyone during the day,
and only flies around when the sun is down.
Now he cannot be found by the animals of the
land and the birds of the sky.

In his dark cave, Bat thinks to himself, "By trying to be on both sides, I ended up on neither side."

That is why Bat flies at night.

The Ant
and
the Dove

An ant went to the bank of a river to quench its thirst, and lost his balance and fell into the rushing waters.

He thought to himself, "This is the end of me."

A dove sitting on a tree next to the river plucked
a leaf and let it fall into the water close to the ant.

The ant climbed onto the leaf and floated safely back to land.

Shortly after that, a birdcatcher came and stood under the tree, and laid a trap for the dove, which sat napping in the branches.

The ant, seeing what was going on, crawled up
to the birdcatcher and stung him in the foot.

In pain, the birdcatcher threw down his trap
and let out a large yell.

The noise woke up the dove and she flew
away safely.

Aesop, a slave in ancient Greece, is famous for his fables: short tales that illustrate truth about life and human nature. Among the common phrases made popular by his fables: "Don't count your chickens before they hatch," "Look before you leap," and "sour grapes."

Many Aesop Fables had morals or lessons.
There is a moral to each of these stories.
Can you match the moral to the story?

- He who is not one thing or the other has no friends.

- One good turn deserves another.

- Trouble tests a true friend.